GRANDPA'S GIFT

Fiona Lumbers

SIMON & SCHUSTER
London   New York   Sydney   Toronto   New Delhi

The City had been home to me for three weeks and four days. Buildings that towered over us replaced the wide open spaces of the home I'd had to leave behind. I missed it.

For Dad, who always shows Sonny and
Teddy the everyday fantastic!

And special thanks to Jane and Holly
for helping me to find the magic in this story.
FL

SIMON & SCHUSTER
First published in Great Britain in 2021 by Simon & Schuster UK Ltd,
1st Floor, 222 Gray's Inn Road, London WC1X 8HB • Text and illustrations
copyright © 2021 Fiona Lumbers • The right of Fiona Lumbers to be identified
as the author and illustrator of this work has been asserted by her in accordance
with the Copyright, Designs and Patents Act, 1988 • All rights reserved,
including the right of reproduction in whole or in part in any form • A CIP
catalogue record for this book is available from the British Library upon request
ISBN: 978-1-4711-6656-3 (HB) • ISBN: 978-1-4711-6657-0 (PB)
ISBN: 978-1-4711-6658-7 (eBook)

As we walked through the concrete maze,
Grandpa took my hand. "I have a surprise
for you," he said.

Grandpa's pace slowed.
As the rain fell in sheets, we took shelter
beneath the awning of a crooked shop.
"We're here," he said.

The window was dusty and full of things that looked like they were unwanted and forgotten.

A little bell tinkled as Grandpa pushed open
the door and disappeared into the shop.

I followed.

I'd never seen anything like it – shelves stretched from floor to ceiling. Boxes balanced upon boxes like circus performers!

I looked around.

Everything was old

and drab,

dusty and tired.

As I flicked through a book,

something caught my eye . . .

"Look, Grandpa!"

Grandpa smiled as he walked towards me.

"Wait until you see what I have to show you," he said excitedly as he slowly uncurled his hand to reveal . . .

. . . a boring,

grey . . .

stone!

"It might just look like a boring, grey stone to you,
but when I was younger, about your age, my grandma told me
beauty and magic can be found in the most unexpected of places.
You just need to look for it."

Carefully, Grandpa prised open the rock . . .

. . . and it filled the shop with a thousand stars.

It was SO beautiful.

Outside, the rain had stopped and the sun was poking through the clouds.

The rock felt safe and warm in my pocket. I stopped to tie my shoelaces and as I crouched down . . .

I noticed a flower growing through a crack in the pavement.

There was a whole world
just beyond my view.

We stopped to eat our lunch,
which we shared with some birds.

A small bird pecked around my feet,
picking up a crumb in its beak.

It flew up into the air, higher and higher.

As I looked up I saw rooftop jungles
framing birds and beasts carved out of stone –
a whole city in the sky!

The city continued to surprise me,
around every corner,

behind each door,

beneath every
fountain . . .

and high up above.

I could feel
the magic of the city
all around me.

As I followed the rainbow,
a small ball bounced and
landed at my feet.

"Can you throw it back,
please?" a voice said.

I stood on tiptoes and there behind the wall was the most amazing playground.

Wow.

"Come and join us!"
the voice shouted –
so I did!

We flew and spun, tumbled and turned, and when
it was time to leave, we promised we'd play again tomorrow.

As we walked home, Grandpa and I talked about the magic
of the city, how it is full of surprises,
    and how when you pause to look,
    you can find beauty everywhere.

We were surrounded by the everyday fantastic,
and for the first time in three weeks
and four days, I felt hopeful.

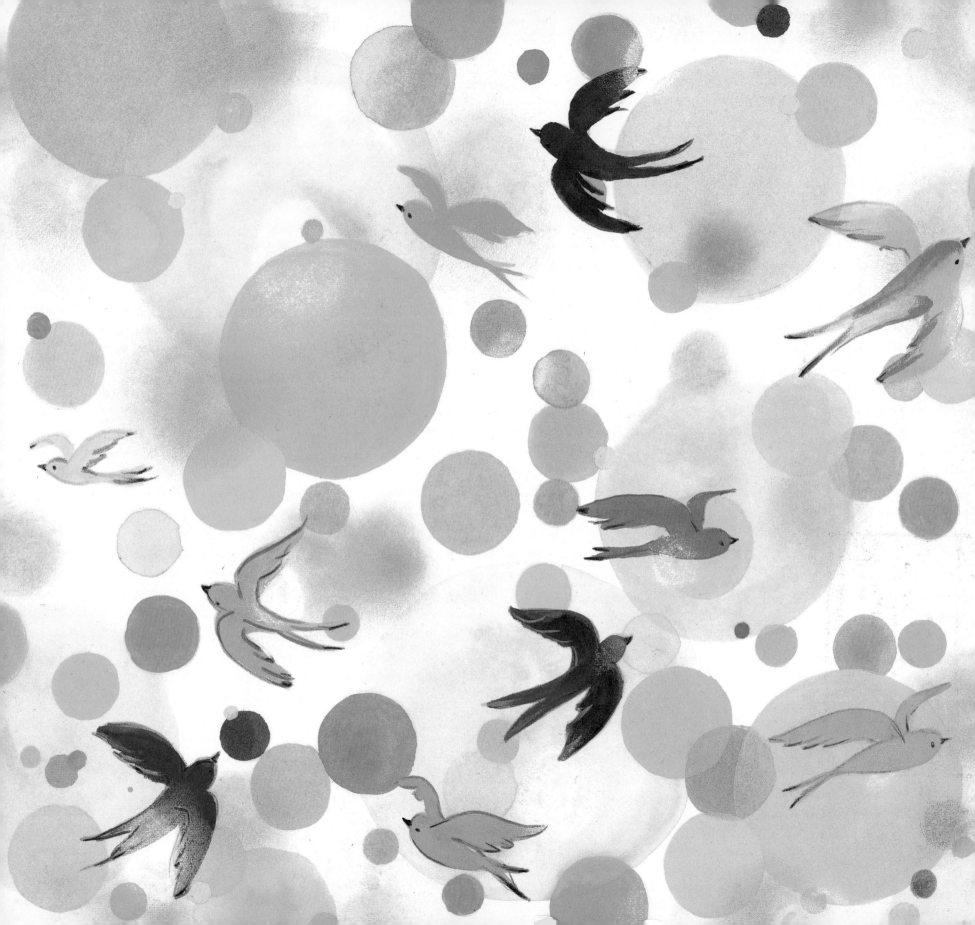